HOPE
THE 'HIP' HIPPO

Produced by:

FriesenPress

Suite 300 – 852 Fort Street
Victoria, BC, Canada V8W 1H8

www.friesenpress.com

Distributed to the trade by The Ingram Book Company

Dedication

This book is dedicated to our Mia, our Abby, EdyAnn, Aleena, Alexa, Kylee, Maisie, Lucy, and every other child who suffers with hip dysplasia. As well as their families who will walk this road with them.

It is offered as a tool to other parents to hopefully aid in their efforts to prepare their child for some of what may lie ahead in their healing and recovery process.

It is our hope that our little story will help you explain things in a way that your child will understand, and that it may remove a tiny bit of the 'scary' from what you will go through.

Please know that having another 'hip' family to walk this road with you is something we both feel is absolutely critical. Please, do not try to do this alone. And, please do not ever feel that you are.

You are in our hearts and prayers. With love,

Gina & Julie

Abby & Mia
Our two
beautiful butterflies

For more information, please check the RESOURCES section at the back of the book.

Forward

This is a wonderful book that is written in a way to help children understand what is happening to them. All too often we forget the child's perspective, but this book bridges that gap and should be read to every young child who needs treatment for hip dysplasia.

Thank you Gina and Julie for writing this book and for helping advance the efforts of the International Hip Dysplasia Institute.

Charles T. Price, MD, FAAP, FAAOS,
Professor of Orthopedic surgery
Director of the International Hip Dysplasia Institute.
Orlando Florida

Hi! My name is **Hope**.

I love to walk, run, jump, play and dance!

Dancing is my most favorite!

I can do the Cha-Cha,
the Merengue,
the Tango and
my favorite, BALLET!

OUCH!

Lately though, when I do those things, my legs start to hurt me…*a lot*.

I don't like it when my legs hurt. It always makes me cry.

Then, my Mommy or Daddy will come and rub my legs for me. It always helps for a little while.

Today, Mommy,Daddy and I are going to go see our friend, Dr. Kindly.

I love to visit my friend! He always tries to make me feel better. I'm sure he can help my pain go away.

Dr. Kindly is always so nice, and is always very happy to see me!

I told Dr. Kindly all about my legs hurting me, and he said,
"well, let's take a look and see if we can't make it all better!"

Dr. Kindly looked at my legs.

Then, he squished them up and pulled them straight out…and squished
them up…and pulled them straight out. Then he moved them all around!

It didn't hurt, so I just closed my eyes and pretended that I was dancing around!

Dr. Kindly said that my hips were so special, that he wanted to take a picture of them!

He called it an "x-ray". Ok, hips, smile pretty for the picture!

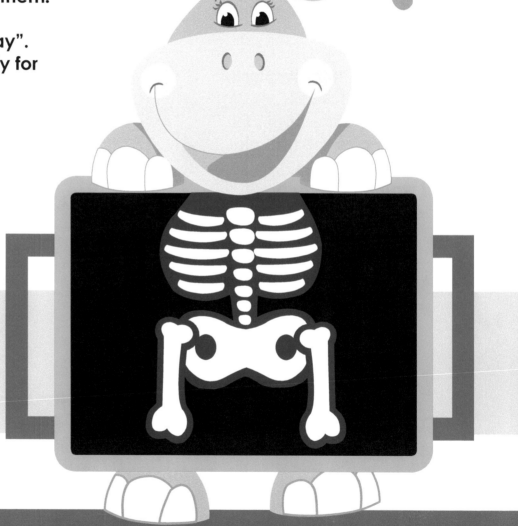

Dr. Kindly showed the x-ray pictures to my Mommy and Daddy, and he looked a little sad. He said that my hips didn't grow right, and that is why my legs hurt.

He said I have "hip dysplasia".

But, he said that he could fix them and make me feel all better! He said in order to fix them I would have to have an operation.

Dr. Kindly told me not to be scared, because he was going to let me sleep all the way through it!

Mommy and Daddy seemed sad now too. But, then they smiled and said, "We're so excited! You are going to feel so much better, when it is all over!"

When the day of my operation arrived, we woke up very early to go to the hospital.

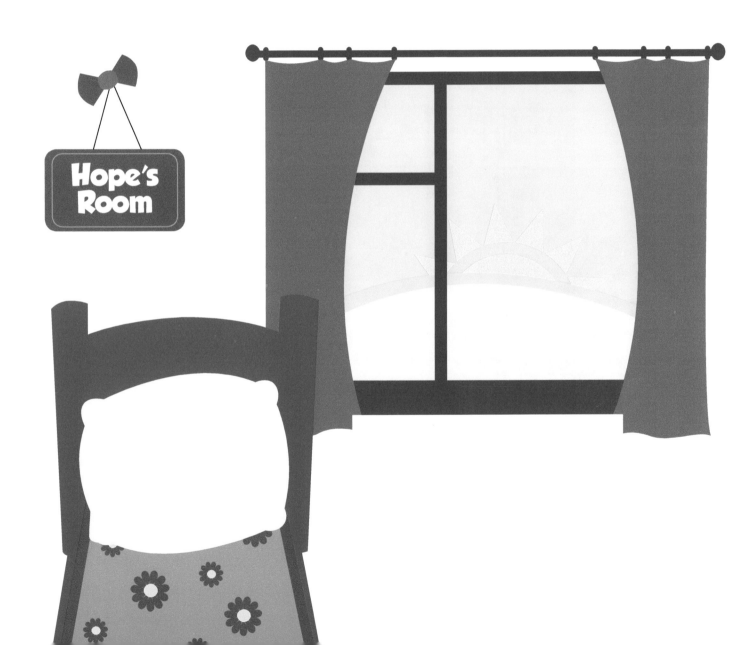

We gathered up my favorite pillow, blanket and teddy bear and away we went! We didn't even have time for breakfast! Dr. Kindly said I could have something to eat and drink after he fixed my hips. I couldn't wait to have some juice!

HOPE

At the hospital, the nurse gave me a brand new nightgown and a VERY cool bracelet with my name on it! Everyone who saw it said, "Hi Hope!" Because of my bracelet, everyone knew my name!

I felt like a

Princess !

Then, the nurse came and took me for a ride, while I was still in my bed!!!

Wheeeee! Away we went down the hall! This was fun!

Dr. Kindly came in to see me and gave me my special medicine. He told me I could go back to sleep now. I was really happy about that, because I was so tired.

When I woke up, I saw Mommy and Daddy smiling at me! But, I felt different. And, suddenly I was a little scared. I said, "Mommy, what happened to me...I'm stuck!"

Mommy said, "No, sweetie, you're not stuck,.Dr. Kindly fixed your hips and now, you are wearing your super special, extra 'cool', cast!" It is called a "spica cast", and mine is a pretty shade of green! Mommy said we could decorate it any way I wanted!

Mommy said I had to wear it for a while, because my hips are very tired and wanted to sleep. I thought that was a good idea!

zzzzzzzzzzzzzzzzzzzzzzZZZZZZZZ

Sleep sweet, hips, so you can feel better!

While I was at the hospital, I got balloons and cards and visits from family and friends! They let me watch movies, play games and drink all the juice I wanted!

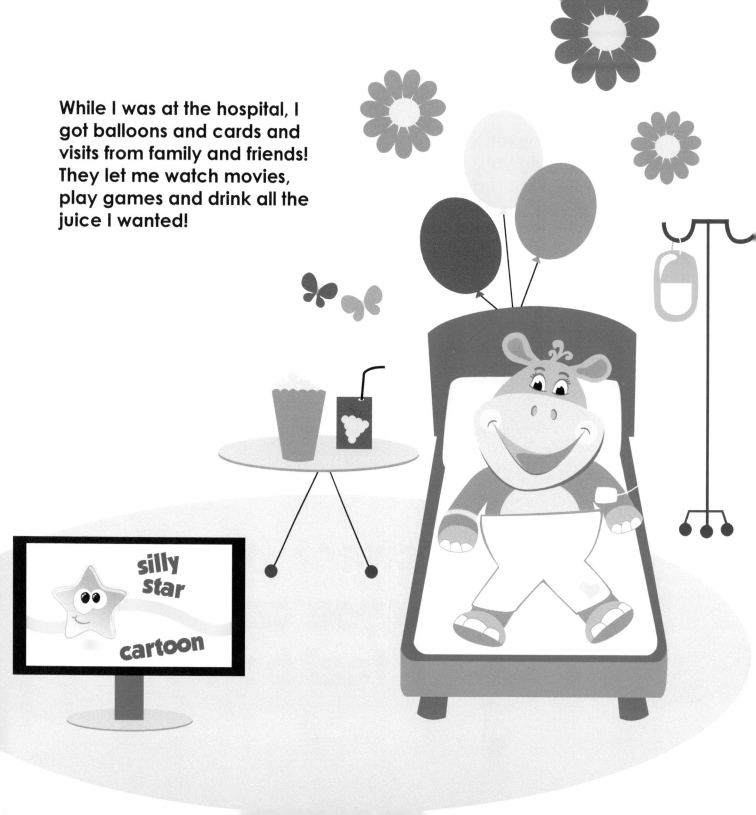

silly star

cartoon

My Daddy even took me for a ride in a wagon through a beautiful park! I loved the blue sky, the butterflies and all the flowers! It was so much fun!

A few days later, I got to leave the hospital...
They even let me wear my cast home!

tweet tweet.
welcome home!

At home, while my hips slept, I let my arms play! My daddy made me a very cool "spica" table so I can sit up in my cast. At my table I can draw pictures, I read books, I colour in my colouring books, I clap and sing songs...why, I even know how to make shadow puppets now!

My hips needed to sleep for a long time! So long, that my cast got all worn out! It was all dirty from me playing in it all the time!

After a few weeks, Dr. Kindly said that we would have to give me a brand new cast for my hips to finish sleeping in. This meant that I get to go back to the hospital, but only for a little while! Then, I was right back home and back to playing!

Sure, there were times when my cast made me itch a little bit and sometimes made me hot, but Mommy and Daddy were right there to fix me up!

We used a special cast "cooler" to keep me cool, and Mommy even used her rubber spatula to scratch my back!

giggle!
that tickles

There were even a few times when I began to get upset because I wanted so much to get up and walk around. I just wanted to play and dance. Even on those days, when my cast made me sad or angry, Mommy and Daddy would let me do something extra special like read a new book, and they would always give me lots of hugs and kisses. They always made me feel better!

Finally, it was time for my cast to come off. You know something? I am a little sad. I had started to feel good in my cast!

Then, Daddy reminded me that when we take the cast off, I can learn to walk and run and play and dance again! I was very excited!

Dr. Kindly brought out his very special cutter, to cut my cast off! He said not to be scared, because it wouldn't hurt.

It didn't hurt, but it sure made a lot of noise! It was loud…VERY loud! I just knew that loud cutter was definitely going to wake my hips up! I hope they don't wake up 'grumpy'! I was a little scared, but I tried to stay very still, and before I knew it, my cast was off!

I tried to move my legs, but you know what? My hips were still asleep! Wow, they must be REALLY tired! Mommy said they would wake up soon, not to worry.

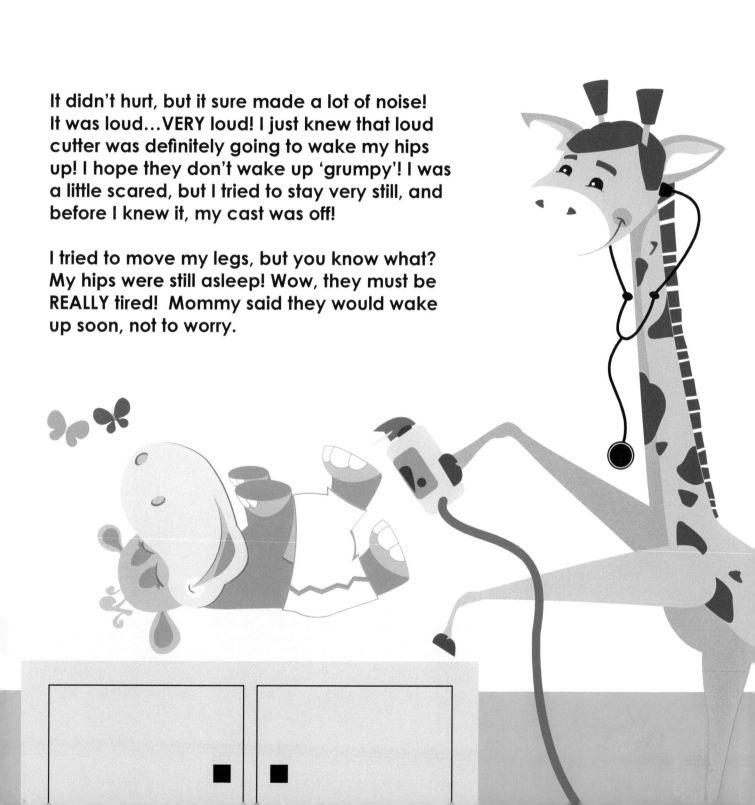

Dr. Kindly gave me a "harness", it was kind of like a special pair of pants. It didn't hurt at all, and my hips even seemed to like it!

Made for: Hope

As time passed, I wore my harness, I practiced moving my legs, and little by little, I felt my hips were waking up!

Yay! "Good Morning, hips...you've been asleep for a long time!"

Now that my hips are awake and, my legs are able to move, slowly, I am learning to walk, run, jump, play...and dance!

And, my legs don't hurt me anymore!

JUMP!

I know that I will have to go back to let Dr. Kindly take more pictures of my hips every so often. I may even have to go back to the hospital, in case my hips start to hurt me again.

But, I also know that I don't have to be scared, and that whatever happens, Dr. Kindly along with my Mommy & Daddy will be right there to love me, take care of me and make me feel better!

And, now…if you'll excuse me…

I am going to dance.

Resources

International Hip Dysplasia Institute (IHDI):
A wealth of information for every stage of the process, as well as
a wonderful place to find and connect with other "hip families" –
http://www.hipdysplasia.org

Also visit –
http://www.git-r-donefoundation.org.
An organization created by "Larry The Cable Guy" which supports
the IHDI, and hip dysplasia research and awarness.

On Facebook:
Hip Dysplasia (DDH) – Children Facing Surgery or Spica Casts:
A great group for meeting others and gaining support –
https://www.facebook.com/groups/Hiptoddlers/

Plus check out –
"One Hip World" https://www.facebook.com/onehipworld

Mia's Miracles:
Mia's journey – https://www.facebook.com/miasmiracles

Blogs:
Mia's Miracles –
http://www.miasmiracles.blogspot.com

Abby's Bilateral Hip Dysplasia Story –
http://www.abbysbilateralhipdysplasiastory.blogspot.com

Messages from the Mamma's

From Mamma Gina:

I want to thank God for all that He is...for all that we are because of Him...and for not leaving our sides for an instant! With all that I am, all that I have, and all that I become, I am yours.

To my Mia: You are my hero and my champion! We are "in it to win it" angel, and Mamma loves you more than you'll ever know. I love you allover!

To my best friend and husband, Michael: You are my life and my love, and together we are unstoppable. We will love our Mia through this, and somehow, God will bring us through stronger than ever! I love you, always!

To everyone on "Team Mia"...our family and friends: It is you who have loved us, supported us, prayed for us, lifted us up and carried us through. Each of you a blessing and a gift, and we love you! Thank you for choosing to be a miracle for us and for our Mia. We carry you in our hearts!!

To Julie: I shudder to think what this would have been like without you by my side. Thank you, my dear friend!

I love you!

From Mamma Julie:

First and foremost I need to thank my God for his loving kindness and patience with me. Proverbs 3:5-6 (NIV) "Trust in the LORD with all your heart and lean not on your own understanding; in all your ways submit to him, and he will make your paths straight." Or as I hope in Abby's case that he makes her hips straight!

To my family and friends...I don't know where to begin! Thank you for all the meals, renting of car seats, wagons, toys, cards, movies, spica chairs, bean bag chairs, words of encouragement, hands of help and friends to play with both Abby and Evan! Mom thank you for telling me at the beginning of all of this, "whatever you do Julie, make her not hate this." For those are the words I have tried to live by. It takes a village to raise a child...thank you all for being part of our village!

Thank you Paul (my husband), for putting up with me and for loving me just the way I am :). And to my Evan! thank you for being such an understanding, loving and caring big brother for Abby!

Gina. In July against my normal judgment I responded to a stranger's post on line from the bottom of my heart. In the weeks and months that have passed "I thank my God upon every remembrance of you" Philippians 1:3(KJV) for your strength, non-judgmental and unconditional support and love I feel from you! I don't know where I would be without you! From one Mommy's heart to another; thank you for being there!

Abby, my sweet pumpkin...let's dance!

Acknowledgments

Cara and Dan Whitney – For breaking through the darkness and shining
a light on hip dysplasia! Their pioneering efforts have given us all a home in the
International Hip Dysplasia Institute. We are all so very grateful!

Dr. Charles Price, Ms. Susan Pappas and everyone at the International Hip Dysplasia Institute.
Thank you for your love and support of **HOPE** and for your dedication to
hip dysplasia research and awareness. You keep us moving forward!

Adrian Stumpf and everyone with Larry the Cable Guys Git-R-Done Foundation for
their love and support of **HOPE** and for their relentless efforts to further hip dysplasia awareness
and research by supporting the International Hip Dysplasia Institute.

Dr. John Heflin and his staff at Pediatric Orthopedics Associates. The Jay family
would be completely "lost at sea" without you to navigate us through these scary
waters. We are so grateful and you are always in our hearts.

Dr. D. Peterson and the staff at McMaster Children's Hospital; for your kindness and
knowledge our hearts give thanks! – The Beattie's

To the entire staff of Children's Health Care of Atlanta at Egleston in
Atlanta Georgia and McMaster Children's Hospital in Hamilton Ontario;
Thank you for taking such good care of us!!

And very Special Thank You to our dear friend Cherie Turner for all of your love,
support, talent and for bringing **HOPE** alive! We could not have done this without you.

Wear your support! Wear it proud...
just like **HOPE**!

To order your awareness wristband,
please visit **www.hipdysplasia.org.**

Search keyword "wristband".

Some of the proceeds from
the sale of this book go to the
IHDI to further research,
education and awareness!

Printed in the USA
CPSIA information can be obtained
at www.ICGtesting.com
LVHW060742251024
794735LV00002B/41